Published by Hachette Partworks Ltd
ISBN: 978-1-908648-33-4
Date of Printing: January 2012
Printed in Singapore by Tien Wah Press

HIAWATHA

Disney
hachette

Hiawatha was a plucky little American Indian who lived on the banks of the River Gitchee Gumee. What he wanted most in the whole wide world was to be just like his father – a great hunter and a brave warrior, who knew all the secrets of the river and the forest.

But it isn’t easy to become a great hunter and a brave warrior. One day, Hiawatha made up his mind – he would go into the forest with his bow and arrow and get some practice!

Hiawatha hopped into his birch-bark canoe and began to paddle. As he glided along the river, he could hear the rustling of the trees and the lapping of the water.

"Minne-wawa!" said the pine trees.

"Mudway-aushka!" said the water.

Hiawatha was excited to be out in his canoe. He skimmed along the river and came to a thundering waterfall. He slipped behind the wall of water without getting a single drop on his head!

Further along the river, he came to a whirlpool. The churning water tugged at his little canoe and spun it round and round. But Hiawatha paddled hard and managed to escape.

Hiawatha knew he'd have to face adventures like this if he wanted to be like his father. To be a true hunter, he must go into the dark forest and track down a squirrel, a rabbit, a deer... or even a great big bear!

He cruised up to the bank and stopped. The plan was to get out of the canoe just like his father – first he'd put one foot on the land, then he'd look around for danger, and finally he'd step off the canoe onto the river bank.

But, oh no... disaster! The current caught the canoe and whisked it away. SPLASH! Hiawatha plopped into the water.

On the river bank, the forest animals couldn't help laughing at poor Hiawatha.

Hiawatha was furious. He clambered out of the water and charged after the animals.

"How dare you laugh at the great hunter!" he yelled at three tiny squirrels.

The squirrels scampered up a tree and were soon safe from the little warrior. Hiawatha looked down and spotted some footprints.

Hiawatha heard a strange, clicking noise. Was it the clacking of sharp teeth? Had he woken up some terrible beast?

Hiawatha followed the clicks and found himself face to face with... a grasshopper!

He aimed his bow and arrow... and then his trousers fell down!

"Oh no!" he cried, very embarrassed.

As he scrambled to pull up his trousers, the grasshopper made his getaway.

The animals were still laughing!

Hiawatha set off again. This time, he was determined to catch something! Soon, he came across a family of fluffy rabbits.

The little Indian gave chase, but all the rabbits got away – all except for the tiniest baby.

The baby rabbit hopped on to a tree trunk. There was no escape from the fierce hunter!

"Yippee!" cried Hiawatha. He began to whoop and stomp around. This was the hunting dance of the proud Gitchee Gumee!

He crept closer and closer to his prey, aiming his bow and arrow. The poor little rabbit was trembling with terror! But then, guess what? The brave hunter's trousers fell down again!

Hiawatha dragged up his trousers and took aim again. But by now, the poor little rabbit had started to cry. Slowly, Hiawatha lowered his bow.

The relieved little rabbit scampered off to rejoin its family.

Maybe Hiawatha wasn't cut out for hunting after all. He couldn't even shoot an animal!

Hiawatha glared at his bow and arrow.

"If I can't use you, I don't need you!" he yelled. And he snapped the bow and arrow in two.

Then Hiawatha heard laughing and clapping. He turned and there were the animals of the forest, giving him a big cheer. If he wasn't going to be a hunter, he could be their friend!

But Hiawatha was ashamed of his failure. He ran off into the heart of the forest.

He sat down on a tree stump, his head in his hands. “I’ll never be a great hunter and a brave warrior like my father,” he sighed.

Suddenly, Hiawatha had an idea.

"Maybe I can be a great tracker instead! I'll follow the animals and get to know them. Then they can lead me to the best grazing grounds, with lots of fruit and nuts!"

Then he looked down and saw more footprints. BIG footprints!

He got down on his knees to look at the prints. Then he put his ear to the ground, listening for noises, just as the men of his tribe did. He started crawling along the trail.

With his head down, Hiawatha didn’t notice he had a new companion. A baby bear was sniffing the ground alongside him!

BONK! Hiawatha and the bear clashed heads.

Both of them looked up and screamed.

The cub scuttled off, as quick as he could.
But Hiawatha wasn't on a hunting trip any more – he just wanted to make friends!
"Hey, come back!" yelled the little brave. "Don't worry, I won't hurt you!" But the frightened bear kept on running.

Hiawatha saw the baby bear hiding behind a big rock. But was it really a rock?

No! When Hiawatha climbed up on top of it, he saw it was covered in fur. Rocks aren't furry! And they don't rumble and shake, either, or roar!

The rock was really a huge bear. She was the cub's mother! She had been enjoying a nap, and wasn't pleased to find Hiawatha on her back!

Hiawatha tried to hang on, but the bear arched her back and he slid off. He grabbed her nose and held on tightly.

“GRRRRRR!” roared the angry bear. She shook her head and Hiawatha lost his grip. He started to run.

The beavers sent out a message by thumping their tails on a tree trunk. Soon, all the forest animals knew that their friend was in danger.

Two raccoons stretched out a long vine and the mother bear tripped over it. CRASH!

The beavers gnawed through a tree trunk. Now Hiawatha could cross the river by raft!

But the bear was close behind. She leapt off the bank and tried to grab the raft. SPLASH!

Hiawatha was flipped into the air. He grabbed a branch and climbed high into a tree.

But the bear was determined. She climbed out of the river and set off up the tree.

Hiawatha was perched at the top. He wasn't feeling very brave now!

The beavers got to work on the tree trunk.

The bear was just about to sink its claws into Hiawatha when the tree began to shake. It toppled over, sending the little Indian flying.

Hiawatha was grabbed by a family of possums, who were swinging from a nearby tree. They whisked him clear of the bear, who landed with a loud CRASH!

Meanwhile, the squirrels had built a little cart, and found a baby deer to pull it. It was time to get Hiawatha back to his canoe so he could go home.

The animals stood on the river bank as their new friend paddled away in his canoe.

And that was the end of Hiawatha's first and last hunting trip. Maybe he would never be a great hunter, or even a brave warrior, but he would make a fine tracker. And most importantly, he was a wonderful friend to the animals of the forest!